VIKING KESTREL
Viking Penguin Inc., 40 West 23rd Street
New York, New York 10010, U.S.A.
Penguin Books Canada Limited, 2801 John Street
Markham, Ontario, Canada L3R 1B4

First published in 1989 by Viking Penguin Inc.
Published simultaneously in Canada
Set in Sabon.
Printed and bound in Italy
Created and Produced by Sadie Fields Productions Ltd,
8, Pembridge Studios, 27A Pembridge Villas, London W11 3EP

1   2   3   4   5   93   92   91   90   89

Do I Have To Go Home?

Karen Erickson and Maureen Roffey

Viking Kestrel

My friend's birthday party is so exciting.

Cake. Ice cream.

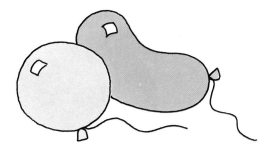

Games.

Presents.

I will never go home. No one can make me.

But now the party's over.

It's time to go.

I don't want to.

My friend's Mom says I can
come over and play again.

She says this is not my
only chance to go to a party.

She says I am a very nice guest.
Nice guests are always
invited to zillions of parties.

I can't wait until the next party.
Look. I can go home even when
I don't want to.
I can do it.
I did it.